FINAL
CUT

FINAL CUT

MARTY CHAN

ORCA BOOK PUBLISHERS

Published in Canada and the United States
in 2022 by Orca Book Publishers.
orcabook.com

Library and Archives Canada Cataloguing in Publication
Title: Final cut / Marty Chan.
Names: Chan, Marty, author.
Description: Series statement: Orca anchor
Identifiers: Canadiana (print) 20210346833 |
Canadiana (ebook) 20210346841 | ISBN 9781459834187 (softcover) |
ISBN 9781459834194 (PDF) | ISBN 9781459834200 (EPUB)
Classification: LCC PS8555.H39244 F56 2022 | DDC jC813/.54—dc23

Library of Congress Control Number: 2021948709

Summary: In this high-interest accessible novel for teen readers,
a bullied teen plots the ultimate revenge.

Orca Book Publishers is committed to reducing the consumption of
nonrenewable resources in the production of our books. We make
every effort to use materials that support a sustainable future.

Orca Book Publishers gratefully acknowledges the support
for its publishing programs provided by the following agencies:
the Government of Canada, the Canada Council for the Arts and
the Province of British Columbia through the BC Arts Council
and the Book Publishing Tax Credit.

Edited by Tanya Trafford
Design by Ella Collier
Cover photography by Getty Images/Prostock-Studio
Author photo by Ryan Parker

Printed and bound in Canada.

25 24 23 22 • 1 2 3 4

To Brad Smilanich, my

movie-recommending guru.

Chapter One

"Run!" I shouted. "Full speed, Maya. Go, go, go!"

My best friend sprinted across the schoolyard as she looked back at the empty track field. Suddenly she tripped and fell to the grass, barely breaking her fall with her hands. Maya scrambled across the ground, panting.

"This way," I yelled. "Come on!"

She swept her long black hair out of her face and looked my way, her eyes wide with fear. She struggled to climb to her knees, then tried to stand up.

"Ow!" she yelped as she took a step. She hopped on one leg. "My ankle. I think it's sprained."

"Ignore the pain," I cried. "Run!"

Maya limped ahead, looking over her shoulder. "Someone help me."

Before she could take another step, the world went dark. I looked up from my camera. Denise had blocked my shot and ruined my take. She was the monster queen of our middle school and could destroy a student's life with just one rumor.

"Excuse me, Denise," I said. "Can you step out of the way?"

"Oh?" Denise said, dusting off her denim jacket. She didn't move an inch. "I didn't know that you were in charge of where I'm supposed to stand."

"*Piggy* bothering you?" a voice called from behind me.

I turned. If Denise was the monster queen, her boyfriend was the beast jerk king. Cole cracked his knuckles and grinned. His braces gave him an evil silver smile.

"The name's Mason," I said.

"Right, *Piggy*." Cole threw his arm around Denise and gave her a kiss on the cheek. "This loser bothering you?" he asked.

"Yeah, he's telling me where to stand," Denise said.

"Seriously?" Cole said. "You think you can tell her where she can go? You know it's the twenty-first century, right? My girl can do what she wants. What are you doing anyway?"

"It's none of your business," I said. "You have the whole field you can use. I just need this spot for another five minutes."

Cole let go of Denise and took a step toward me. "Want to move me, *Piggy*?" He had called me Piggy ever since we started playing rugby together. We were the same size, but he didn't like that I could run faster. He was captain and decided to make me his punching bag for the rest of the season.

He'd given me the nickname when he learned my dad was a cop. Cole was the main reason I quit the team.

"Leave Mason alone," Maya shouted as she ran toward us, her limp gone.

Denise laughed. "*Weeve him awone.* Speak English much? Why don't you go back to China?"

"I'm from Vietnam," Maya said.

"Wherever," Denise said. "Go back to where you came from. Don't stink up our school."

I gritted my teeth. I could take these jerks teasing me, but I couldn't let them make fun of my friend.

"Maya was born here," I said. "If you bothered to get to know her, you wouldn't be so ignorant."

Denise narrowed her gaze at me. "What did you call me?"

"You heard me," I said.

"Take it back," Cole said.

"I can handle this, Cole," Denise said as she walked toward me.

"You know I'm livestreaming all of this right now?" I said, moving closer to the camera on the tripod. "Everyone probably heard everything. Maybe even the principal."

Denise glared at me. Her short red hair made it look like her head was on fire. She stared right into the camera.

"Some people can't take a joke."

Cole rolled up beside her on his longboard. "Yeah, Denise. Snowflakes are so sensitive these days. Hello, butt sniffers. Hope you're enjoying the show."

Denise laughed. "Sniff away."

He sniffed the air. "Ah, fresh butt hurt from all poor little snowflakes." He kicked his board up into his hand. "Come on, Denise. Let's go back to where *we* came from."

As he turned, his longboard smacked into my tripod and sent the camera flying. I lunged to catch it. Too slow.

"Oops. Sorry about that," Denise said.

They laughed as they walked away. I rushed to check my camera. Nothing looked broken.

"Is it okay?" Maya asked as she knelt beside me.

"Yeah. Don't let those jerks get to you," I said.

"Not the first time I've heard that insult. Mason, I can't believe they thought you were livestreaming," Maya said.

"Hey, what they don't know can't hurt us," I said.

"True. Want to do another take?"

"No, I think I got enough from you before they showed up."

"Come on. I think I have another take in me," Maya said. "I can make my limp look more real this time."

I shook my head and started to unscrew the camera from the tripod. "No, we're losing the light." I pointed up at the clouds blocking the sun. "I can finish shooting our movie tomorrow."

I handed Maya the camera and turned to watch Denise and Cole halfway across the field.

"I wish they could get a taste of what they dish out," Maya said as she put the camera into its carrying case.

"Ha. They wouldn't be able to handle it," I said. "I'm so glad I'm getting out of this city."

"You looking forward to going to Toronto?" she asked.

"Anywhere is better than here," I said. "I get to escape from these jerks."

"Take me with you?"

"Of course. I need my leading lady for all my horror movies," I said.

She smiled. "When do you leave?"

I folded up my tripod. "Dad's already there. Mom's dealing with the movers. We drive out Monday, so tomorrow's my last day."

"I'm going to miss you, Mason. Who's going to turn me into a movie star?"

"Well, maybe this will be your big break. Just one more scene, and I should have all I need," I said.

"And if it's a hit, I get to be in the sequel, right?" she joked.

"Of course. I'll fly back, pick you up in a limo. We can jet off to Hollywood," I said.

"Well, I'd better get my own trailer and assistant."

"Nothing but the best for you. I should make Denise and Cole the monsters," I said.

"Too scary." Maya made a face.

I laughed. "Yeah, we don't want to freak out the—wait. That just gave me an idea."

"What?" she asked.

"Maybe they're not right for our movie, but I can make them stars of their *own* movie."

She leaned in. "Ooh, sounds like a horror classic in the making."

I grabbed the camera case from Maya. "No, I'm thinking of this one as more of a comedy."

"Mason, what do you have planned?" she asked.

"You'll see," I said as I stuffed the gear into my backpack.

Chapter Two

The next day my latest video hit the internet. All the kids at school were buzzing about the clip. I felt like I was on the red carpet at a movie premiere, but I couldn't tell anyone that I was the director of this viral video.

Still, I could enjoy their comments on the sly. I lurked behind a group of ninth graders as they watched my video on a phone.

On the screen, Denise's and Cole's faces were pasted onto the butts of two pit bulls.

Cole said, "*Snowflakes are so sensitive these days. Hello, butt sniffers. Hope you're enjoying the show.*"

A bark came from Denise before she said, "*Sniff away.*"

Cole sniffed the air. "*Ah, fresh butt.*"

The clip ended with a big fart sound effect and a loop of Cole and Denise repeating their last lines.

"*Sniff away...Ah, fresh butt....Sniff away... Ah, fresh butt....Sniff away...Ah, fresh butt.*"

One boy howled with laughter. "Play it again! That's hilarious."

When Cole and Denise had interrupted my shoot, the camera had caught everything they said. All I had to do was use an effects filter to stick their faces on two dog butts.

"They're buttheads!" a girl said with a laugh. "'Sniff away.' Hilarious."

More students crowded around to watch the clip. I cracked a smug grin and enjoyed the rave reviews.

Cole and Denise walked down the hallway. I slipped to the back of the crowd and watched as Cole pushed his way to the middle, smiling.

"What's so funny?" Cole asked. "Let me see."

Silence fell on the crowd.

Denise raised an eyebrow. "Why are you all looking at us like that?"

"*Sniff away*," came Denise's voice from the phone, followed by Cole's voice saying, "*Ah, fresh butt.*"

Everyone burst out laughing.

"What is that?" the real-time Denise asked.

Cole grabbed the phone and watched the clip. Denise's voice rang out. "*Sniff away.*"

"Who posted this?!" Cole growled.

His voice sounded from the phone. "*Ah, fresh butt.*"

Laughter filled the hallway. Denise pulled Cole away before he could punch the kid with the phone. I giggled to myself and walked away. Mission accomplished.

I couldn't wait to find Maya to show her my new masterpiece. She was sitting at her desk in our homeroom, staring at her phone. Off to the side a few students were chatting.

"Maya, I have to show you something," I said as I headed to her desk.

Her face lit up as she held up her phone. "You mean this?" she asked.

My movie played across the screen. I beamed.

"It's amazing," she whispered.

I took a bow. "Thank you, thank you, thank you. No, seriously, thank you."

"Cole must be losing his mind," she added.

"Saw him in the hallway," I said. "He's definitely not happy."

"You'd better be careful."

"I'll be long gone before they figure out it was me," I said.

Maya shook her head. "He'll *know* it was you."

"I don't think he's smart enough. But what will it matter if I'm halfway across the country?" I said. "Anyway, forget them. Look at what I have for our final scene."

I reached into my backpack and pulled out a prop knife and a severed hand, complete with bloodstains. Maya's eyes grew wide as she grabbed the hand from me.

"Where did you get that, Mason? It looks so real," she said.

"Bought it online," I said. I pulled out a ketchup squeeze tube and waved it in the air. "Throw a little corn syrup and red food coloring together, and you have a bloody good time."

"Nice," she said. "So I'm assuming this is going to be what's left of you."

I nodded. "Yup. After searching everywhere for me, you learn that the killer got to me first."

"Got to hand it to you," Maya said.

I rolled my eyes. "You're too young to be making dad jokes."

"Yuk, yuk," she replied. "So when do you want to shoot?"

"Today after school?" I suggested. "I've got about two hours before I have to get home and pack."

"You haven't started packing yet? Talk about leaving things to the last minute."

I grinned and tucked the hand and tube of fake blood back into my backpack. "Got pretty much everything in here. Camera, batteries and special effects. What more does a filmmaker need? Let's meet by the fence after school."

"Okay," she said. "This is going to be our best movie yet."

My last day of classes was all joy, no tears. While I'd miss Maya, I already had plans for a horror movie about her being trapped in a Google Meet. We didn't have to be in the same city to film it.

Plus, hearing the constant loop of Cole and Denise's butthead video everywhere I went was sweet revenge. Payback for all the times they had bullied me. Students were repeating the lines to each other in the hallways. Denise hid in the girls' bathroom for most of the day. Cole was shaking down kids to find out who had made the meme. I couldn't think of a better way to end my time at this school. Nothing was going to bring me down.

As I watched the clock ticking down to the end of science class and the end of my time at this school, my phone buzzed.

I reached into my pocket. A text from Maya. My mouth dried up as I read the words on the screen.

They know it was you.

Chapter Three

I felt like a victim in a horror movie. Denise and Cole were the killers chasing me down. I had to get home before they caught me. Forget waiting for the school bus to roll out. I had to make a run for it. I slipped my backpack over both shoulders and ran for home.

The first few blocks, I kept staring over my shoulder to make sure Cole and his pals weren't on my trail. If this were a horror movie, I should be tripping on a blade of grass right about now. I didn't, but my legs felt like jelly, and my T-shirt was soaked with sweat.

My best bet was to duck down a side street and then make my way to somewhere I could catch a city bus. The only problem was, I didn't know how many people Denise and Cole had rounded up to help look for me. They could be around any corner. I hoped my head start was enough to buy me the time I needed.

I reached a busy street with shops and restaurants and scanned the area for a bus stop. Ah, yes! I spotted a bus parked across the street and down a block or so. Its door was open. But before I could cross, Denise's friend Nadia rolled out on her mountain bike. She skidded to a stop between me and the bus. Nadia towered over almost every student and some of the teachers, and she had a mean streak.

"Hey, Mason," she said with a sneer. She reached into her pocket and pulled out her phone.

No way was I going to wait for her to rat me out. I turned and sprinted in the other direction.

"Get back here!" I heard her shout.

The backpack slapped against my sweaty back as I sped away. I hoped my camera would be okay, but that was the least of my worries. I could hear the whiz of Nadia's bike wheels on the sidewalk as she closed in.

I nearly slammed into an old couple coming out of a store. The man shook his fist at me.

"Sorry!" I yelled as I looked back.

Nadia nearly knocked over the woman, barely zipping around her at the last second.

"Ring your bell!" the woman yelled. "Damn kids!"

Nadia ignored her and poured on the speed toward me.

"Leave me alone!" I screamed as I ran down the sidewalk. "I didn't do anything to you."

"Denise is my friend!" Nadia yelled. "You're going to pay for what you did!"

I kept running, but I knew it wouldn't be long before she caught me. All she had to do was call her friends and I'd be done for. Ugh. Why had I uploaded the video last night? I could have waited until I was free and clear of the school and those jerks before posting it. *Could have, should have, would have.* I could hear my mom's voice in my head and picture her wagging finger.

"You're dead meat!" Nadia shouted.

She was so close now I could smell the rubber from her front tire. I swore she was going to pop a wheelie and roll right over my back. I changed course and ran across the street. A truck screeched to a stop in front of me. *BEEEEEEPPPP!*

"I almost killed you!" the man behind the steering wheel yelled before punching his horn again.

I dodged more traffic and somehow managed to get to the other side. Nadia on her bike would have to wait for the traffic to clear before she could cross. At least, that's what I hoped. I headed along the row of shops, gasping for air. My lungs burned. My backpack loaded with my camera and special-effects gear was slowing me down. Even after two seasons of rugby, I couldn't keep up this running pace. Why had I brought all my stuff with me today? *Could have, should have, would have.*

I heard the whiz of a bike's wheels.

"Mason!" Nadia shouted.

She had caught up to me again. Home was too far away, and I couldn't outrun her bike. I spotted a clothing store with an open door. I slipped inside and closed the door behind me. I ducked behind a rack of women's tops so I could catch my breath. Through the window, I watched Nadia skid to a stop and hop off her bike. She looked down the street, then pulled out her phone. Cole and Denise wouldn't be far behind.

A young clerk was folding clothes in the middle of the store. She caught me looking her way and flashed a smile. "Welcome to Junipers. May I help you?"

"Um, is there another way out of this place?" I asked.

Her smile never faded. "I'm afraid not. But everything is 20 percent off today."

I glanced out the window at Nadia texting. Time was running out.

"My name is Melanie, if you need anything," the clerk said. "Anything at all, I'm here for you."

"Thanks," I said. "I'll just look around."

"Be sure to ask for me," she said.

Melanie was pushy. I guessed she needed a sale.

"Remember, everything in the store is 20 percent off," she said.

I nodded and pretended to search through the rack of clothes in front of me.

Buzz. The door opened and Nadia entered. She blocked the entrance.

I was trapped.

Chapter Four

I had to get out of the store before Denise, Cole and their goons showed up. But Nadia was one of the best players on the rugby team, and no one ever got by her.

I shuffled through the maze of clothing racks and display tables until I reached the back of the store. An older woman with glasses sat behind the register. She was doing a crossword puzzle.

I coughed lightly to get her attention.

She lowered her paper and looked at me above her black-rimmed glasses. "May I help you?"

"Um, that girl," I started, but I didn't know how to explain my problem. I felt like I was in third grade and about to snitch on another student.

"Young man, if you're looking for something, our sales staff can help you," she said.

"I think I'm being followed," I said, nodding toward Nadia.

The woman looked over at the door,

then adjusted her glasses to get a better look at me.

"Well, well, well. Aren't you the heart-throb?" she said.

"No, I mean that girl won't leave me alone," I said.

The woman put both hands on the counter, the many silver rings on her bony fingers glinting in the light. "Honey, you should be flattered a girl that pretty has taken an interest in you."

"No, she's not...I mean, she's not interested in me. She's trying to—"

She cut me off with a wave. "Enjoy it while it lasts, sweetie. Must be your full head of hair. My husband used to have hair like that." She sighed.

"No, you don't understand," I said.

She chuckled and picked up her crossword again.

No one in the store was going to help me. I slipped away from the counter and hid behind one of the display mannequins. I peeked out to get a look at Nadia. Maybe she had left her post, and I could duck out. No luck. Still at the door. No doubt Cole and Denise were on their way. If I didn't leave now, I was done. But I'd need a bulldozer to clear Nadia out of the way. Or maybe...

I had an idea.

I hurried over to the pushy sales clerk folding pants nearby.

"Excuse me, Melanie?" I said.

Melanie flashed her fake grin. "Welcome to Junipers. May I help you?" Her smile faded when she saw it was me.

"We talked a little while ago," I said. "I think I need your help now."

Melanie placed the pants on the table. "Of course. What can I help you with?"

I lowered my voice and turned my head to the door. "Not me. Over there. By the entrance. That's my sister. She's looking for something. She asked me to look around, but to be honest, I have no idea where it is."

"I am sure I can help," Melanie said. "What does she need?"

"Well, she's embarrassed about this, so she might not admit it…but she needs a new bra," I said. "She's only worn sports bras and wants something, you know, a bit more frilly."

Melanie nodded, taking the situation very seriously. "Not a problem."

"If you ask her about bras, she'll pretend she doesn't know what you're talking about. But trust me, she really wants one."

Melanie patted me on the shoulder. "Don't worry. She'll be in good hands."

"Thank you," I said.

"You're such a thoughtful brother," she said.

"Don't tell her I told you," I said. "She'll kill me."

"It'll be our secret." Melanie winked at me as she mimed pulling a zipper across her lips. I slipped back behind a clothing rack.

Melanie headed straight to Nadia. I was close enough to hear everything.

"Welcome to Junipers," said Melanie in her annoying perky voice. "How may I help you today?"

"Uh, I'm waiting for someone," Nadia said, glancing around, probably trying to figure out where I'd disappeared to. "I'm not here to buy anything."

"Oh, I understand. But maybe you'd like to take a look at a few of the things we have to offer. Everything is 20 percent off today. We have a lovely selection of girls' tops. And other things."

"I'm not interested," Nadia said firmly.

"Of course," Melanie said. "Because you haven't seen what we have to offer yet.

Come over here. I think I have just the thing a girl your age needs."

"Thanks, but no."

Melanie took Nadia by the arm and guided her away from the door as she said, "Sometimes what a woman needs is something to make her feel pretty."

"Wait. What?" Nadia asked.

"And we have some lovely options right over here," Melanie said as she guided Nadia toward a rack of bras.

"What?!" Nadia said, trying to break free of Melanie's iron grip. "No way. I'm not looking for bras."

Melanie smelled a sale and wasn't about to let Nadia go. The pushy sales clerk kept herding the red-faced Nadia to the lacy bras.

I didn't want to miss the fun, but my escape route had opened up. I sprinted to the front of the store and shouldered the door open. Fresh air blasted my face. Freedom!

I glanced through the giant window and then at Nadia's bike. She probably wasn't going to be leaving the store anytime soon. But if she did escape Melanie, she'd catch up to me in no time. I yanked off my backpack and searched the bag. Ah, perfect. I pulled out the prop knife. It wasn't sharp like a real knife, but it had a tip that worked well enough. I stabbed the front tire of the bike a few times until...*hiss*! Yes! For good measure, I deflated her back tire too. I slipped the knife back in my pack and searched the street for the nearest bus stop.

I jogged away from the store. Home was just a bus ride away. No sign of a bus stop, but I wasn't about to give up. Just then I saw Denise rolling on her board on the other side of the street. I tried to duck behind a trash can on the sidewalk, but she spotted me.

"Mason!" she howled from the other side of the street. "You are rat chow!"

Chapter Five

I zipped around the corner and poured on the speed. The traffic might delay Denise for a bit, but not forever. I sprinted to a restaurant and tried to open the door. Locked! The sign read *Open at 5*.

Behind me Denise yelled, "Mason!"

Damn. I'd thought it would take her longer to get across the street. But she was rolling toward me on her board. I scrambled along the sidewalk, looking for another place to hide. Nothing on the street was open. The clack of Denise's skateboard wheels grew louder as she closed the gap between us.

I zipped past a couple of guys hanging around outside a bar, nearly slamming into one of them.

"Watch it, kid!" a burly guy with a beard warned.

"Sorry," I called back.

I turned into the alley beside the bar and headed to the other end. The smell of stale beer and garbage filled my nose. I had to put some ground between Denise and me. I leaped over a puddle.

"Get away from me!" Denise screamed.

As her words sunk in, I slowed down, confused. I thought she wanted to kill me.

"I mean it. Get away!" I heard her yell.

I looked back. The man with the beard stood in front of Denise. She was trying to roll away, but he kept his foot on her skateboard. A skinny guy, clearly a friend of the bearded guy, was circling around behind her.

The survivor in me screamed, *Run away!* But I couldn't tell if I was saying that to myself or to Denise. I moved closer to the trio.

"Come on, sweetie," the bearded guy said. "Let us buy you a beer."

"Not interested," Denise said.

"Not a beer girl?" he said. "That's okay. How about I get you something stronger?"

"Get off my board," Denise said.

"Ooh, this one's got some fire," he said to his skinny friend. "You like to party? We do. Come in. We'll show you a good time. My name's Mike, but you can call me whatever you want."

"I'm not old enough for the bar," Denise said.

"Then I guess we'll have to get some beers to go," Mike said.

He leaned closer to Denise. She stepped back, but the skinny friend blocked her escape. Part of me thought Cole and his pals would show up any second to chase off the drunks. Another part of me thought

Denise should suffer for all the times she had bullied me.

Mike grabbed Denise's arm and pulled her toward the entrance. "Come on. We'll have fun."

"Let go of me," she said.

He didn't seem to hear her.

The noble part of me won out. I unzipped my backpack. Blood tube. Nope. Knife. Not a great idea. Severed hand. Maybe. Ah. My camera. Perfect. I pulled out the camera and aimed it at the three as I walked closer.

"Got anything to say for the six o'clock news?" I shouted.

The two men stepped back from Denise.

"Mind your own business, kid," Mike growled.

I held the camera up, aiming it at the three of them.

"Put the camera away," his skinny friend warned. "We weren't doing nothing."

"I'm livestreaming all of this right now," I said. "I'm sure your bosses or your families will want to know what kind of men you are."

The bearded man started toward me. "Give me that camera!"

"It's all streaming to my channel," I said as I backed up. "You can't erase the internet."

The skinny friend grabbed Mike's sleeve. "Leave it, man. He's not worth the hassle."

"Screw it," Mike said. "I'm going to knock the teeth out of this punk."

I kept backing up with my camera aimed at Mike. Behind the two men, Denise jumped on her board and rolled off. I had bought her the time to get away. Now I had to get out of the alley with all my teeth still in my mouth.

"Beating up a kid is going to make you the star of my livestream and the police report," I said.

The skinny man grabbed Mike. "I can't afford to lose my job."

Mike stopped. "Little punk is going to get everything he deserves."

"Forget it. Not worth it."

Mike growled, "I'm just going to teach this kid a lesson."

"Let's go back into the bar," the skinny man said, "and I'll buy you a beer."

"You paying? That's a first. Buy me two," he said.

"Sure, sure. Whatever, Mike. Let's just get going."

I lowered my camera, sweat pouring down my forehead. Mike glared at me while his friend walked into the bar.

"I see you sniffing around here again, that camera is going to catch some real action. You feel me?" he threatened.

I nodded, ready to bolt if he tried to grab me. He staggered to the door and went inside. I started to breathe again. I didn't think I had taken a breath the entire time.

I put the camera back into its case, slipped it into my backpack and turned to head out. A shadow blocked the other end of the alley.

Cole cracked his silver grin at me. "Going somewhere, *Piggy*?" he asked.

Oh great. If I'd left Denise to the bar goons, I would have been halfway home by now. I zipped my backpack shut and slung it over my shoulder. Time to run. Again.

Suddenly hands grabbed me from behind. For a second I worried that the bearded man had decided to come back for revenge. I carefully looked over my shoulder. It was Min, one of Cole's best friends.

"You're not going anywhere," Min said,

standing so close I could smell his garlicky breath.

I slipped out of his grip and shoved him back as I bolted for freedom. Cole's other pal, Darin, stepped out from behind a dumpster and slammed his fist into my stomach. I gasped and fell to the pavement, clutching my gut. I landed right in a puddle.

"We ain't done with you," Darin said.

I tried to catch my breath as my hands sloshed in the puddle. In the reflection of the water, Cole towered over me. He grabbed my hair and hauled me to my feet.

"You're going to pay for that video," he said. "And I'm going to enjoy every minute of it. Every. Damn. Minute."

Chapter Six

Min and Darin dug their fingers into my flesh as they held my arms. I could still smell Min's breath. Darin groomed his upper lip with his other hand. His mustache was barely there, but he liked to draw attention to it.

"Give it up, man," Min said. "You have the same number of mustache hairs as you did last week."

"I wasn't counting. I was…itchy," Darin said, pulling his hand away from his face.

Cole pulled a pair of scissors from his back pocket and grinned as he snipped invisible hairs just in front of my nose.

"Want to know what I'm going to do with these, *Piggy*?" he asked.

I had seen enough awful teen movies to know exactly what he had planned. But showing fear would only make it worse. "Work on the art project you never finished in kindergarten?"

Min elbowed me.

"Keep it up, funny man," Darin said as he squeezed my arm.

Cole snipped the scissors, moving even closer to my face. "You're going to be my new art project. I think I'll call it *The Bald Pig*."

His pals laughed. I jerked to one side, trying to break their grip. No good. They were too strong.

"Piggy, you are going to regret ever making that movie," Cole said.

"I don't know what you're talking about," I said.

"Don't even try to play me. I know it was you."

"How do you know?" I said. "Anyone could have made it."

Min yanked my arm to get my attention. "Next time you brag to your girlfriend, maybe check to see who's around first. I heard you taking credit for the video in the classroom this morning."

I bit my lip. They had me.

"Now you're going to pay for what you did," Cole said as he pulled an electric shaver from his other pocket. He flipped the switch on the razor and let it buzz as he waved it over my head.

"Get that thing away from me," I ordered.

He smiled and clicked it off. "Don't want to waste the batteries. I'm gonna need it for the full shave. Now, Darin."

Suddenly pain exploded in the back of my knee. I went down on the hard pavement. My knees scraped against the hard pavement. I struggled and squirmed to break free, but Min and Darin held on tight.

"No, no, no!" I shouted.

The thugs laughed as they held me down.

"Help!" I yelled.

Darin clamped his hand over my mouth. I bit into his palm. Hard.

"Ouch!" he yelped. "Cole, I get a turn with the shaver after you."

I tried again to pull free. I looked up. A middle-aged couple walked past the open alleyway.

"Help!" I screamed.

They stopped for a second. The woman jumped back, surprised. The man squinted at us as he moved closer. His partner tried to pull him back, but he kept walking. "You okay, kid?"

I was about to answer, but Min cut me off. "He's fine."

"I want to hear from the kid," the man said, taking another step toward us.

"We're helping him up," Darin said. "He fell."

"Leave them be, Harry," the woman called from the mouth of the alley.

Darin and Min squeezed my arms so hard I thought they were going to break them. I winced as they hauled me to my feet.

"Well, kid?" the man asked. "You really okay?"

"I don't feel so good," I said, fighting the pain in my arms.

Cole stepped in front of me. "It's okay, sir. My cousin had a few too many drinks.

Thought he could handle more than he could. Serves him right for sneaking into the bar with fake ID."

The man eyed me up and down for a second. "You know you shouldn't be doing that, kid?"

His partner called to him, "He looks fine, Harry. It's none of our business."

Harry shook his head. "You kids should know better."

"That's what I keep telling them, but do they listen? No," Cole said. "Don't worry. I'm going to take good care of my cousin."

The man nodded and turned to join his partner at the end of the alley. They headed away. I opened my mouth to scream again, but a sharp blow to the back of my head shut me up.

"Try that again, Mason. I dare you," growled Darin.

I clamped my mouth shut.

"Too many people here," Cole said. "We have to find a quiet spot to shave this pig."

"Where?" Min asked.

Darin cracked a grin. "The skate park. You know the shack just on the other side of the main ramp? No one ever goes there. Plus, when we're done, we can parade Mason in front of all the skaters."

Cole laughed. "Perfect. Let's shave this piggy."

Chapter Seven

No way was I going to let these jerks shave my head without a fight. I dug my feet into the pavement and backpedaled. Min and Darin twisted my arms behind my back and shoved me toward the end of the alley while Cole texted on his phone.

"Damn, this guy's heavy," Darin said.

Min grunted. "You're telling me. Come on, Mason, pick up your feet and walk."

No way. I let my body go limp. Min and Darin grunted and groaned, trying to hold me up. They hooked their arms under my sweaty armpits, but I wasn't about to make it easy for them.

"Ugh," Darin complained. "He's so heavy. Give us a hand, Cole."

Cole looked up from his phone screen and growled, "Piggy, pick up your feet and walk, or I'll start shaving you right here."

I gritted my teeth. "Forget it," I grunted. "You're going to shave me either way."

He narrowed his eyes at me as a cruel

smile slid across his lips. "Shave or *cut*. Your choice."

I refused to show Cole I was scared. I clamped my lips shut and glared at him, daring him to shave me right there.

Instead he slammed his fist into my stomach. "What's it gonna be?"

I couldn't answer because I couldn't breathe. Cole clenched his fists and wound up for another punch.

"You walking, or am I cutting?" he said through gritted teeth.

"Walking," I gasped.

"Good decision," Cole said.

He walked out of the alley as Min and Darin hauled me after him. I hated this guy more than anyone I'd ever hated before.

Many people streamed past us. Most of them were office workers heading home at rush hour. No one bothered to look my way. Cole walked in front of me, blocking anyone's view of me. Not that anyone would care if they did see me. They were more into whatever was on their phones.

I glared at Darin. "You always do what Cole tells you?"

"Shut up," Darin said.

"This make you feel big?" I asked. "Ganging up on one guy?"

Min laughed. "You had it coming to you."

"For what?" I said. "A video. After all the things Cole and Denise did to me?"

"Next time, just shut up and take it," Darin said.

"Like you?" I said.

Darin elbowed me in the ribs. "I ain't no pushover."

After a few blocks, the sound of the skate park reached my ears. Almost there. I dragged my feet and went limp. No way would Cole try to cut me on the open street. This was my last stand. Min kicked the back of my knee while Darin slammed his elbow into my ribs.

"Keep moving," Min ordered.

I refused, trying to turn into a bag of wet cement. Finally the thugs dragged me past the park and toward the wooded area near the high ramp. The trees and bushes would provide all the cover Cole needed to shave me bald.

Just in front of a locked green shack, Denise waited for us. She glanced up from her phone and put it away.

"Took you long enough," she said to Cole. "I've been here for twenty minutes."

Cole shrugged. "There's a reason I call him *Piggy*."

"Still going ahead with the plan?" Denise asked.

"Yup. I'm going to love making his head into a cue ball," he said.

She gave me a sideways look. "You sure about this, Cole?"

"You bet. He deserves this." Cole pulled out the scissors from his back pocket.

"Yeah…" she mumbled. "I guess."

"What's wrong with you?" Min asked. "Going soft?"

She shook her head. "Shut up, Min. I'm not talking to you. Not now. Not ever. And chew some gum. Your breath reeks."

Min sheepishly covered his mouth and sniffed his own breath.

Darin said, "Mason's going to get what's coming to him."

In every slasher movie, one victim always gets a face-to-face with the killer. The victim usually begs for their life, hoping the killer will change his mind. He never does. I wasn't about to beg Cole for anything, but I also wasn't about to let the beast jerk king shave me bald. With four against me, I couldn't fight them all off. I needed something to even the odds or chase them off. Then a wicked idea formed in my mind. My backpack!

"Do whatever you want to me," I whined. "Just don't break anything in my bag. I paid a lot of money for my camera gear."

Cole's pals laughed. "You think we care?" Min asked.

Darin added, "Yeah, we'll be super careful with your stuff, won't we?"

"Do it, Darin," Cole ordered.

Darin let go of my arm, ripped my backpack off and threw it to the ground.

"No," I yelled as I pulled away from Min's grip and fell beside my bag. Then, before anyone could stop me, I crawled on top of my backpack and cradled it in my arms.

Min and Darin tried to pull me onto my feet, but I was curled around my bag.

"Don't touch me!" I howled as I unzipped the main pocket.

Min grabbed my hair and pulled. I reached inside and groped for something to help me. My hand wrapped around a tube.

Darin tore the bag from me, and Min hauled me to my feet by my hair. I yelped in pain as I pulled away, leaving him with a tuft of my hair as I staggered toward Cole. Instead of trying to stop, I picked up speed and slammed right into the bully, squeezing the tube at the same time. Something wet oozed all over my stomach and hands.

I staggered away. Denise gasped while Darin and Min jumped back. Cole's eyes went wide with shock.

I stared at the blood on my shirt and hands, then looked up at Cole and his scissors. Blood had splattered his rugby top.

"What? No. I didn't...." Cole tried to explain, trying to rub the blood out but smearing it farther across his shirt.

"Oh jeez, Mason's bleeding," Denise said.

"The scissors," I said. "You stabbed me."

I staggered past Cole and made my way out to the park, where the skaters stopped.

"I didn't do anything," Cole said.

"Help me," I moaned, holding up my bloody hands to show off the red wound blooming on my Dawn of the Dead T-shirt. I turned to point at Cole and his goons, and then I fell to the ground.

Chapter Eight

From my angle on the ground, I could see skaters rushing toward me. I moaned and rolled over to see Cole, Min and Darin frozen in place and staring at me.

"Killer," I said, lifting a shaky finger at Cole.

"Get him!" a skater yelled out. Others echoed the call.

Darin grabbed Cole's arm. "Oh man, oh man, oh man," Darin said. "Let's get out of here."

Min had already turned and fled.

"Wait for me!" Darin called as he sprinted after Min.

The skaters vaulted over my body and charged at Cole. He dropped the scissors and backed up.

"I didn't do anything. I swear," he said.

"Someone call the cops!" a skater yelled.

"No. It was an accident," Cole tried to explain, holding up his hands, which were also splattered with blood. "Seriously. It wasn't me."

The skaters closed in. Cole turned, but Denise stood in his way.

"Let's get out of here!" he barked, but when he reached out for her hand, she turned away and stepped aside.

"Suit yourself," he said as he ran away.

The skaters rolled after him on their boards.

Denise ran toward me and knelt down. "Are you okay?" she asked.

I glanced around. The skaters were gone.

"What are you doing, Denise?" I asked.

"Checking on you," she said.

"Why do you care?"

"Back at the bar," she said. "You didn't have to help me. Why did you?"

"What does it matter, Denise?" I said.

"I can handle myself."

"Okay, next time I'll leave you alone," I said, sitting up.

"Hey, be careful. You've been stabbed," she said.

The girl who had bullied me all year long actually had a heart? I was stunned.

"I should call an ambulance," Denise said, nervously chewing her bottom lip. "You're bleeding pretty bad."

I cracked a grin. "No, you don't have to call for help."

"But you're bleeding," she said.

"Yeah. I can clean that off." I dragged my bloody hand across my mouth and licked it.

"Gross!" Denise said.

"It's okay, Denise. It's corn syrup and red food coloring," I said.

"What?!"

"Fake blood," I explained. "I was going to use it for the movie I was shooting."

"So Cole didn't stab you?" she asked.

I shook my head. "No. I just pretended he had stabbed me. Beats getting shaved."

She nodded. "You know Cole probably just wanted to put a scare in you. I don't think he would have done it."

"Probably? Not good enough," I said. "I like my hair where it is."

"He gets carried away sometimes," she said.

"Yes, I noticed. Well, I guess I should let

the skaters know that I'm okay." I started to get up.

Denise held out her hand to help but stopped when I showed her the fake blood on my palms. "Mason, that video stunt of yours went too far. Everyone's been mocking me all day long."

"Yeah, well, I guess it was overboard," I said. "Sorry. I didn't think it would go through the whole school. Now you know how I feel most of the time when you make fun of me."

"So…I guess that might make us even," she said. "Sorry I was a jerk to you. Fresh start?"

"Um…okay. I guess I should tell you

that this was my last day at school," I said. "I'm moving to another city."

Her eyes widened. "So the video was your goodbye gift?"

"Yeah. Kinda," I said.

She shook her head. "You got moves, Mason. I'll give you that much."

"We okay?" I asked.

Denise stared at my bloody shirt. "If we aren't, you'd probably frame me for murder, so I think it'll be better to stay on your good side."

I laughed.

"Good luck with your new school," she said. "Maybe I'll sub your channel and check out the horror movie you're making."

"That'd be nice," I said.

"Then I'll troll you until you regret you ever uploaded the thing," she said.

My stomach twisted into a knot.

She smiled. "Now we're even. See you around, Mason."

"Not if I see you first," I replied.

Denise walked away. I rubbed my bloody hands on my shirt, grabbed my backpack and headed for home. I hoped Cole and his buddies would think twice before they picked on the next student. Part of me was sure they wouldn't change their ways, but another part thought that if Denise had heart, maybe they did too.

I had no plans to stick around to find out. Still, it would have been fun to show up at school and film the look on Cole's face when he saw I was alive…or maybe I'd come back as a zombie. No, a ghost. Wait, what about…

So many great ideas for my next blockbuster movie.

Acknowledgments

Michelle, you are the first reader of all my manuscripts and the first person I ever trusted with my writing. Thank you for all the hours you have spent reading my words. Wei Wong, you are the last reader of my manuscripts, but I trust you to keep me from looking the fool. Thank you for your sharp eyes and your generous heart.

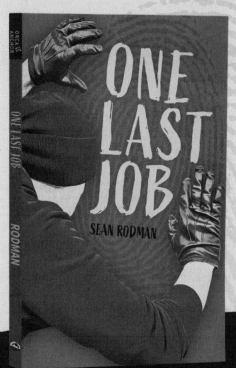

The burglar pulls out a drawer from my grandpa's desk. He shakes it upside down. Papers and pens fall to the floor.

"You want some pencils?" says Gramps. "I've even got pens, if that's what you're looking for."

"Don't make him mad," I hiss at Gramps. The burglar ignores us and keeps on making a mess. He dumps a bunch of files out, papers flying everywhere. Then sweeps a stack of hardcover books from their shelves. He empties kitchen cabinets. Pots and pans clatter across the linoleum.

"He's not very good at this," says Gramps.

"Shut it!" roars the burglar, not looking at us. He's busy tossing clothes out of the dresser onto the floor.

Gramps lowers his voice and leans toward me. "Seriously, this guy is an amateur. And I should know."

Gramps has lived, as he puts it, an "adventurous life." He doesn't talk much about it, and neither do my parents. But I know he had a criminal career that ended with a couple of years in prison.

"How about I save us all some time?" says Gramps to the burglar. "There's twenty bucks in a pickle jar by the door. It's for the cleaning lady. Aside from that, you're not going to find anything here. I've got nothing to hide."

The burglar slowly stands up and turns around. He pulls an old wool sock out of the dresser. There is clearly something hidden inside the sock. Reaching in, he pulls it out. A small wooden box. The burglar sneers.

"Nothing to hide, huh?" he says and tilts open the lid. Gramps swears softly. The burglar lifts up a necklace. It's a thin silver chain with a teardrop-shaped pendant dangling at the end. It catches the light and sparkles like a drop of water.

"That's no good to you," says Gramps. "Seriously, take the money. Take the TV. Whatever. But leave that, all right?"

The burglar takes several steps toward us. "Naw. I'm taking it."

"Back off!" I yell. I spring from the couch,

but the burglar gives me a sharp shove in the chest, sending me to the floor.

Suddenly my grandfather's watery blue eyes turn hard and focused. His voice rattles like a rake over gravel.

"You are making a mistake, son. Leave my grandson alone. Leave the necklace where you found it. Walk away. Take the money by the door. I won't call the cops. Final offer."

The burglar leans down over Gramps. He dangles the necklace in front of the old man.

"You really trying to scare me?" He lunges at Gramps suddenly. Expecting him to flinch. Trying to frighten him. But Gramps doesn't even blink.

"No," says Gramps. "I'm just giving you fair warning. Steal that necklace, hurt my family, and you'll pay." For a moment the burglar hesitates. Then his lips curl into a sneer, and he shakes his head. Then he walks toward the front door. As he passes me lying on the floor, he swings a boot at my chest. The air whooshes out of my lungs, and I gasp for air. The burglar grabs the pickle jar by the door and then slips out the door.

It doesn't take long for me to cut the zip ties off my wrists and free Gramps. I reach for my cell phone.

"Don't do that," says Gramps. He hasn't moved from the couch since the burglar left. He's just sitting there. Rubbing his wrists. Thinking.

"Don't tell the cops," he adds. "And don't tell your parents. Don't tell anyone. We're going to handle this. You and me."

That's when Mom walks in.

Marty Chan is an award-winning author of dozens of books for kids, including *Kung Fu Master*, *Haunted Hospital* and *Kylie the Magnificent* in the Orca Currents line and the award-winning Marty Chan Mystery series. He tours schools and libraries across Canada, using storytelling, stage magic and improv to ignite a passion for reading in kids. Marty lives in Edmonton.